To Cher and Trixie

Text and illustrations copyright © 2007 by Mo Willems.
ELEPHANT & PIGGIE is a trademark of The Mo Willems Studio, Inc.

This book is set in Century 725/Monotype; Grilled Cheese BTN/Fontbros; Neutraface, Fink, Typography of Coop/House Industries

Printed in Malaysia
Reinforced binding

First Edition, September 2007
20 19 18 17 16 15 14 13 12
FAC-029191-17157

Library of Congress Cataloging-in-Publication Data on file.
ISBN-13: 978-1-4231-0687-6
ISBN-10: 1-4231-0687-3

Visit www.hyperionbooksforchildren.com and www.pigeonpresents.com

I Am Invited to a Party!

An **ELEPHANT & PIGGIE** Book

By **Mo Willems**

Hyperion Books for Children / *New York*

AN IMPRINT OF DISNEY BOOK GROUP

I am invited to a party!

It is cool.

Will you go with me?

I *know* parties.

Really?

I know parties.

He knows parties.

zIp!

ZAP!

ZAP!

ZIP!

26

A fancy pool party?

He knows
parties.

ZIP!

ZAP!

ZAP!

zip!

ZIp!

ZAp!

ZIP!

Well, that is a surprise.

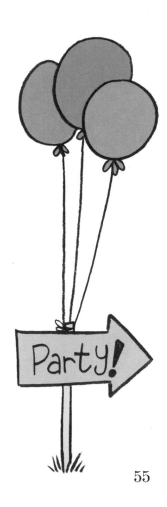

Party!

Have you read all of Elephant and Piggie's funny adventures?